Adventures in the Planes of the Worldmask
Volume Eight: Other Worlds

By Rachael Knight

Dedicated to John,
who is featured in almost every one of these stories in different ways.

A Duel at High Noon

I was born on a world that no longer exists…

My family owned a vast expanse of land at the heart of a fertile valley. I was born there, in the middle of an especially hot summer, and grew up on the ranch my family called home. Miles of rolling plains to run in, racing the wild horses. A deep and crisp river to swim in, fed by the nearby mountains and full of fish to catch. And a stretch of ancient woods to explore to my heart's content, teeming with game and wild mushrooms and berries. It was a perfect place for a child to grow up, with vast golden skies and plenty of room to stretch and breathe.

My Ma and Pa had the kind of love that only exists in fairy tales. You know, the kind where they can't look at each other without a goofy smile… I always knew that my Pa would do anything to make my Ma happy, and she would gladly do the same. They were obsessed with each other. In my foolish youth, I did not realize how rare such love was. Only when I was older did I see that I wanted that sort of happiness for myself as well. Then I became unstoppable in my search for true love. And oh, how the young ladies melted to my charm! But none of them were the special something that I sought after. And none of them stuck around for long…

The ranch had a very successful business to support it, in the breeding and training of winged mounts. Pa's specialty was with hippogriffs, and he made a hefty profit each year by selling his stock to the wealthy men in nearby towns. When I was old enough to learn the trade, Pa began to take me along for these adventures. I was privy to all sales talks, which usually took place around a table in the local saloon. In this way, I learned the finer points of both the art of the business deal and the art of playing cards. Pa would even allow me to gamble with my own savings if I so chose, warning me that he would not be paying for any debts I might incur. But I had a knack for the game, and I generally left with more coin than I started with, much to the chagrin of the older humans and elves I played against.

In the off-season, I worked with my Pa, my uncles, and my brothers to tend the land and to provide meat for our tables. My

Ma and the women would forage in the trees for all manner of seeds and spores for future plantings. And fallen wood would be collected for cooking fires.

We also each took our turn in caring for the animals. Sometimes, this meant shoveling shit from the barn or lugging around buckets of dead rats. But even those chores were rewarded on days when I was tasked with taking the fledglings out for their flight practices. I came to love the sensation of riding, both across the land and the sky. And on the day I became an adult, my father awarded me with a steed of my own.

The ranch flourished with each new season. Even if we found we were short on something, we never went without. There was always enough excess for us to barter with our neighbors, and I came to know everyone in the valley very well as I was generally the one to make the journeys back and forth between the different homesteads. Our trade generally consisted of feathers, grain, mushrooms, and even some of our family's home-brewed whiskey.

But this isn't to say that life on a farm is without its dangers. Wild animals were a common occurrence, some more deadly than others. In particular, the nearby mountain brought griffons down on us on a regular basis. They loved to tear up the barn, hoping to get at the hippogriffs inside. And I became quite skilled in taking them out of the air before they could do any real damage. I had always been comfortable with the gun on my hip, but it was this challenge that encouraged me to turn it into a form of art.

My life was a peaceful one, all things considered. I loved my family. I was friends with my neighbors (Even the ones whose daughters I had propositioned over the years). And I was happy to live in my own little corner of the world as my family had done for generations.

There came a time however, when I was still a young man, that trouble really did come knockin' at our door. One of the nearby towns had been growing steadily for decades. Suddenly, it was more of a city, and those who lived there cared little for the customs and lives of those who lived beyond their walls. It seemed life in the country was growing obsolete, and we faced that realization with a hard lesson indeed...

Pa and I went into the city as usual with the new stock. They were four of the finest beasts we had ever raised on the ranch, proud creatures of a pale gold and dappled through with black. Even selling just one of the four would provide enough profit to carry the ranch into the next season. And we were as eager to get started as the people were who had come to view our latest batch of impressive mounts.

We were nearing a sale with our first potential customer, a wealthy man who was new to the city. He explained that he had a special interest in our ranch and that he had heard great things about our stock. When he requested a closer look at the hippogriffs, Pa was all too happy to grant it to him. But that happiness was short-lived, as the man proceeded to handle one of the creatures a little too roughly under the guise of 'inspection'. I can't be sure what he did, exactly. All I know is that the generally mild-tempered beast screamed and then lashed out at his attacker.

The next few moments went by in a flash that seemed to stretch on for eternity. The rich man tumbled back, untouched despite having obviously harmed one of our animals. And as the hippogriff advanced on him angrily, the man's bodyguards rushed forward and dispatched the poor creature without a second's hesitation. Right there in front of the entire city, our prized beast bled out onto the street while the rich man screamed to anyone who would listen that our animals were untrustworthy and violent monsters.

Despite our reputation for providing upstanding mounts for decades, the man's words held a weight we could not counter. We only managed to sell one of the other hippogriffs, and that one at a mere pittance of a price. We were forced to return home with the remaining two still in hand, and my Pa's face held a new weariness that was never there before. I could see he was worried, and I tried my best to assure him that our next season would be better. We couldn't have a perfect run all the time, after all. Still, it did little to cheer him up, even after we were home.

The next few years were certainly harder. Our solid reputation had been shattered by a single rich man's words. And had it not been for our neighbors, and countless hours tending to our fields, we might have struggled to get by. But we had enough to live, even if we couldn't afford everything we once had, and we managed well enough in providing for ourselves over the long summers.

Then came the day that the rich man came calling at the ranch. He and Pa talked outside, unaware that I was listening in to their conversation. What I heard filled me with a deep loathing for the wretched man.

It seemed his aforementioned interest in our ranch held some truth. He came with an offer to buy our land from us. Enough money to set up the entire family in any town we desired. And he proposed an added bonus of fifty gold for the hippogriff he had cost us.

That alone sent Pa onto the defensive. For a creature such as that, we could have made upwards of two hundred gold. For this man to come forward with such an offer was more an insult than anything else, and he told the man so. He then demanded the man leave his land before things got messy.

The rich man was obviously not happy with this reply. He feigned a smile, gracefully taking his leave. But from around the side of the house, I caught the grimace as he turned away from Pa. And I knew we hadn't seen the last of him. I told Pa as much when I joined him in the yard a moment later. Pa agreed with my opinion, promising that we would all take measures to ensure that the fool did not get his way.

That evening, Pa called a meeting with our neighbors. It didn't take long to find out that the rich man had made the same offer to everyone else in the valley. Most had already turned him down, though some were considering taking the money and seeking better pastures elsewhere. They warned that they had heard of this fellow in the past, and that he was quite single-minded when it came to getting what he wanted. They feared that refusing him now would only cause more trouble down the road. But my Pa was of a different mind. He insisted that he would fight for his home, no matter the cost. And for my part, I was ready to stand with him.

The following months rolled by at a painstakingly slow pace. It seemed the rich man was just as determined as he claimed to be. He hired countless thugs to chase out those who lived within the valley. Gardens were raided. Smoke sheds were burned down. Barns were vandalized and the livestock within, mutilated. Each new week brought more bad news as our neighbors slowly caved under the assault from the man in the city. And once every quarter, the man himself would return. Each time, his offer was smaller and he warned Pa that continued stubbornness would only hurt his family further. Pa put a bullet into the dirt between his fancy shoes in response on the last visit. I'm sure that is what sent the rich man over the edge into full-on insanity.

The evening of their last discussion, the rich man's hired thugs slipped into our back fields and set fire to the wheat. It quickly spread out into the pastures, sweeping over everything and leaving nothing but blackened earth behind. Eventually it ignited the still, which exploded in a wave of heat and light. We were barely able to contain it before it reached the houses. And it was at this point that many of our hired hands chose to leave in favor of life-preservation.

That next winter was especially hard on us. I hunted and fished whenever I could, but we had lost most of our crop and a majority of the seed for the following season. We didn't starve, but we were certainly stretched thin; especially with most of our neighbors fleeing to greener fields. And I understood that we would have to come to some type of solution if we wanted our ranch to survive.

Then the river ran dry before the first snow melts could reach us. It was obvious that the man had paid to have it dammed up. But we could hardly fight against it when he was doing so from land he owned upstream from us. We were forced to rely entirely upon our well for clean water, and there were no more fish to provide meat for our table.

Pa could not let this slight rest. He packed up for a trip into the city, vowing to talk to the man and convince him to stop. I warned him against this plan. Something about the idea triggered alarms in my head. But he was adamant on the issue, placing me in charge while he was away and strapping on his pistol for good measure as he headed out the door. That was the last time I saw him alive…

A courier brought the news of his passing. According to all official reports, Pa was struck by a runaway carriage just inside the city walls. It was labeled a 'tragic accident', but I sensed there was more to it than that. And it came as no surprise to learn that the carriage belonged to the very man Pa had gone into town to confront.

I volunteered to make the trek into the city to retrieve his body. In part, I did this because I knew it was my responsibility. But I also knew that leaving the task up to my Ma would only hurt her further. And I didn't want her anywhere near the man I believed had murdered her husband.

The rich man was waiting for me when I reached the city. He was dripping with false sincerity and sorrow, speaking to me as a child rather than the man I was. I instantly hated him even more. Once again, he offered to buy our land.

"You *are* the man of the house now, after all," he said slyly. "And I'm betting you're a smart one, too. Let me take it off your hands. It would cost more than it's worth to try to rebuild it, anyway."

His words filled me with a fury I had never felt before. I was firm as I gave him my answer. "That land has belonged to my family for twelve generations. My father ran it on his own for sixteen hundred years before I was even born. And I will be *damned* if I throw away that legacy for any amount of your filthy money! The ranch is our home and *my* birthright! So don't you dare tell me what it is worth! You will never have it."

The rich man was far less jovial in the face of my words. "Careful, Boy," he warned. "You could come to regret such a decision..."

But I would hear nothing of it. Whatever he wanted with our land, I would not be toppled like some foolish kid. Pa had been the strength of our family for longer than I had been alive, but now it was time for me to take his place. This battle was far from over, and I refused to go down without a proper fight.

Raids became far more prominent after that. Between myself and the other men of the ranch, we were able to keep our assailants from reaching beyond the outer fields. We made sure there were never any bodies left to rot, and their valuables were all collected and secreted away to be sold in other towns. But this ate up much of our time, and it left the women to handle most of the labor of running the ranch. Even worse, Ma was never the same after Pa died. She just withered away, shrinking in on herself until there was nothing left. Eventually, she refused to speak to anyone at all and did little more than sit in her chair and stare off into nothing. My youngest sister made sure she ate, because she would not do it on her own anymore. And it was almost a relief when she chose to finally follow Pa to the next life, nearly a year and a half after he was buried.

Ma's passing rekindled my rage at the rich man. He had been forced to go about his plans without our land; a fact I soon discovered when I made my first foray out over the valley in almost six months. The devastation I saw there was unbelievable. Our ranch was the single strip of green in all the valley, a veritable island of life in a sea of torn up earth and jagged stone. It seemed the man was searching for something within the land itself.

I hated the sight of the valley so destroyed. It was enough to cement the wild idea that had been bouncing around in my mind. The idea that came to me whenever I was feeling particularly reckless... And I did not hesitate to saddle up once more, for another trip into the city. This time, I would meet the rich man on my own terms.

He was happy to meet with me, of course. Somehow, he had learned of my Ma's passing and he expressed his deepest condolences. I could see through his lies with ease, and I was sure to let him see that. In return, he was quick to try to shift things to business.

"You've reconsidered, have you? Have you finally seen that my offer is better for you? From the looks of your clothing, I would say you've had it pretty rough out there in your valley."

"Cut the crap," I snapped back at him coldly. "I'm not here for your measly offer. I'm here to give you one of my own."

The rich man was a little more reserved as he responded. "Very well. Let's hear it then."

"I'm challenging you. Officially. No stand-ins. No substitutes. Just you, me, and our guns." I took great satisfaction in watching him falter before he could compose himself.

"And what would the wager be?" he asked softly, his eyes carefully calculating.

"Isn't it obvious?" I demanded. "If you win, you get my land."

"And if I lose?" the man prodded slowly. "Do you think I'm the only one standing in your way?"

"Of course not," I answered smoothly. "Cockroaches don't live alone. But if *I* win, I want your entire estate. Your land. Your money. Everything."

This time, the rich man was slower to speak up. "That hardly seems fair..."

"Why not?" I demanded. "You're asking me for everything I have ever known and loved. Everything I have. I'm only insisting upon the same! Seems plenty fair to me."

Not to be intimidated, the rich man forced a laugh. "I will admit, what I seek under your little ranch is worth far more than the land itself... Alright, if this is the only way to make you submit, then I accept your challenge, Boy. But I have to warn you that you have made a grave mistake."

"We'll see about that," I promised him.

"So when are we doing this?"

"No time like the present," I told him with a morbid smile. "Get your affairs in order and meet me outside the West gate at noon."

The rich man was definitely flustered. Beads of sweat formed at his temples and he wiped them away impatiently. “Won’t you need time to inform your family that you won’t be coming home?” he asked weakly.

I knew that was his way of reaching for more time and refused to give it to him. “They’ll know as soon as you’re dead,” I told him confidently. Then I turned on my heels and marched away, leaving him to scramble in preparation for our next meeting.

He showed up, despite my assumption that he would turn tail and run the moment I was out of sight. But I didn’t let my surprise show on my face. And when he unveiled a shining, embellished pistol of the highest quality, I didn’t flinch. After all, a gun is only as good as it wielder. And this man could never match my own skill with my Pa’s old firearm strapped to my hip. Decades of practice filled me with confidence as we faced off outside the city walls. And as the bells rang out to announce the turn of the hour, that old pistol was in my hand in a flash of light and an intake of breath. The silence was broken in a roar of sound. Both guns were fired. But only one hit its mark.

The rich man crumpled, his hand mangled beyond use. His fancy gun had flown far from his grasp as my bullet tore through his knuckles and into his wrist. He dove toward the weapon with a pitiful whimper, but I was far from finished with him.

“I can’t provide any solid evidence, but I know you had a hand in my father’s death,” I growled out. I emphasized my words with a second shot to the man’s torso, throwing him back from his gun in a spray of blood. “Now, you’re finally going to pay for all the pain you’ve wrought… Any last words?”

“Don’t kill me!” the man blubbered immediately. “Please! You’ve won! I’ll give you anything you want!”

But I could still see his free hand inching toward the knife in his boot. I stepped up and placed the barrel of my pistol to the man’s head. Right between the eyes. “I already got what I want.”

BANG!

The rich man collapsed, splayed out in a mess of brains and

viscera. I regarded him without emotion for a moment. There was no satisfaction in the kill. Only a deep seated sense that balance could finally be restored. It was another job I had to do, nothing more... I collected his shiny pistol, strapping it onto my other hip in silence. Then I pulled the deeds to the valley from his coat pocket. The rest of his wealth was quick to follow as the man's assistants produced chests of coin and titles to multiple large homes in various cities. I took it all, my face an unreadable mask, and the first thing I bought was a new set of clothes in the style my Pa had favored. I paid extra to have my family crest sewn onto the back of the duster. Then I returned home to share my victory and to begin the real work.

Between my uncles and I, we were able to track down nearly everyone who once called the valley home. I offered them their land back, free of charge, so long as they would return to help us rebuild. Most agreed on the spot, and together we started by leveling the earth and constructing new homes. The river was freed. The trees and grass were replanted. And I used my new fortune to provide for everyone over the next few years as they resettled into their old lives.

It took nearly three decades to restore the valley to its former beauty, and even then it was never quite the same. But that was all well and good. The people were safe and happy, and my family could at last move on in peace. They all saw me as some sort of local hero. I didn't quite agree. I was just the man who took it upon himself to set things right. I didn't need anyone looking up to me...

There came a point when the money finally did start to run out, and sooner than I liked. I knew the ranch would be okay without me for a time, so I took the opportunity to travel. I decided I could visit the homes I had 'inherited' in the duel. Most were probably far enough away to be more of a hassle to me than anything else, so I reckoned I could pick one or two I liked and sell the rest. The profit from such a trip would no doubt secure my family's future for at least another decade.

Everywhere I went, old associates of the rich man came out

of the woodwork to challenge me. Some believed I had gotten in a lucky shot. Some claimed I cheated. But they all had the same idea, that they could somehow exact revenge upon me for killing their buddy. I faced each of them without flinching, always just a little too quick on the draw for those lazy bastards to match. And I always made sure they were dead, so they couldn't come calling again.

Over the next few years, I sent enough coin and goods back to the ranch to let everyone in the valley live quite comfortably. I kept only what I could carry in my saddle bags, using it for food and drink, and the occasional game of cards.

Though each duel I fought was the result of the other man's challenge, I soon earned a reputation as something of a boogeyman for the corrupt elite. Wherever I went, people knew my face. Countless individuals sought to bring me down, if only for the fame such a feat could bring them. I stood my ground against each and every one of them, and few were lucky enough to land even a glancing hit on me. Soon, I became known by the name Swiftshot, by the common folk.

To these everyday people, I guess I was a blessing. In removing enemies from my own path, I also freed hundreds of others from the oppression of debt. Many were happy to welcome me on sight, and I was generally obliged to accept offers of room and board; especially when a lovely woman was doing the offering.

But even in the midst of the best of times, the time spent away from home began to weigh heavily on me. I began to have nightmares concerning the ranch, and even in my waking hours I could not shake the fear that something new and terrible was coming. I was prepared long before the news reached me that the valley had been raided once again, this time with a magic user working against us. It took nearly four months for the message to get to me, so I knew there was no way I could make it back in time to help in the fight. It was probably already long over. The best I could do was return home to help with recovery.

But it seemed that the universe had other plans in mind,

because I never saw my beloved ranch again. Within the first week of my journey the ground was shaking and the animals fled in panic. Even my ever-stoic hippogriff was struggling to remain calm. A few days later, the sky grew hazy with smoke and ominous storm clouds. And by the time a month had passed, the sun was completely obscured. Great fissures opened up as the ground ripped itself apart. And magma burst up from the core of the world. Cities fell. Millions died. And I fought for every step I took to make it back to the valley.

There was no knowing what had caused it... But my world was definitely coming to an end. I knew that in my heart before I ever set eyes on my home. And seeing what was left of the valley was little more than a final nail in the coffin for me.

The valley was gone, collapsed in on itself and burned away to ash and dust. The hills ended in an abrupt cliff face, from which I could only stare in horror and despair. The forests, the river, the fields... My home. My family, and everyone else I had convinced to come back... All of it gone... And soon, I would be following behind them as my planet died...

Final Defiance

"Miri, do you feel like going out, today? I hear the guards are giving us all an extra hour on the grounds if you're-"

Katai stopped short in the doorway, looking around at the empty room in surprise. The bed was made. The heavy curtains were shut tight on the iron bars that blocked the chamber from the world beyond. The candle on the table by the door flickered in the last few inches of its life. But the person who usually occupied the space was nowhere in sight.

"Miri?" Katai called again. She stepped inside and checked behind the privacy screen in the corner, where Miri usually tucked herself away when she was upset. But the girl was not there either. "Miri?!"

Fear was not something Katai was used to feeling, even in a place like the Blackstone Keep. But the silence of the chamber filled her with dread. Her first assumption was an unpleasant one, and she quickly turned on her heel and marched back out to the communal quarters. If Miri wasn't there, then there were very few other possibilities, and they were the ones she was not ready to face.

Had Carnifax claimed the girl at last? Demon or not, Katai shuddered at the thought. Miri was only half-devil, and had always been a thorn in the side of the Pit Fiend who ruled over the keep. For years, Katai had cared for her, and the thought that he might send her to the Pit after so long... The pain the succubus was experiencing at the thought of losing the girl was unbearable.

Many heads turned as she entered the common room of the harem, where all manner of women lounged amid the cushions. Demons. Devils. Monsters and mortals alike. They regarded her with a mixture of fear and respect; as was to be expected. After all, Katai was the first concubine of their master. She had been here the longest. She was Carnifax's favorite, and she was not someone to take lightly.

"Has anyone seen Miri?" she demanded.

The other women of the harem knew Miri well, though they had always taken care to avoid her. Bound, as the girl was to Katai, she was off-limits to the rest of them. No one offered a response.

Tail lashing, Katai narrowed her eyes and let out a soft hiss. "Does *anyone* know where she is?" she tried again. "Did Carnifax call for her?"

"Carnifax isn't here," a young devil answered with a roll of her eyes.

"What do you mean?" Katai asked in confusion.

"He was called away last night to meet with the King of the Hells," the blue-skinned woman responded dryly. "Didn't you know that?"

Normally, Katai might have been tempted to strike the girl for her insolent tone, but she had *not* been informed of the Pit Fiend's leaving. It didn't surprise her much. Carnifax had been called away before on business; and much more frequently of late to deal with the King. Any other time, such news might have come as a relief to her, as it represented the only true free time that any of them got. But not today...

"He didn't take her with him, did he?" she queried nervously.

"She was with us for our morning excursion," another woman, a rakshasa, offered quietly. She shrank back as Katai rounded on her. "But I don't think she came back in with us when the bell sounded..."

Katai sucked in a breath, her blood running cold as she considered the implications. Miri had been acting strange for weeks. Sullen. Closed off. She had refused to leave the room or to attend breakfast with the others, in favor of hiding in her bed. If she was taking action now, slipping away while Carnifax was out, that could only mean one thing. The girl was trying to run. Katai knew she had to get her back before...

"How long until our Master returns?" she demanded of the room.

A few of the women shrugged, but none could say for certain. A few days. A matter of hours... There was no telling with Carnifax.

Katai growled in frustration and quickly left the room.

Outwardly, she did her best to appear furious, and a part of her truly was. But underneath the anger was a greater emotion, one she was not so used to feeling; terror. As much as she hated to admit it, Katai was deathly afraid for the girl.

She marched down the dark hallways of the keep, heading toward the doors. With each step, her thoughts grew more convoluted and worried. It had been many long decades, centuries even, since they lost Miri's mother to unexplained circumstances. Katai had done the best she could to repair the damages left by Gzifa's absence, but Carnifax was not one to forgive. He blamed Katai for the loss of his favorite plaything, and had replaced the drow woman with her daughter in the blink of an eye. Miri's life had been torment ever since, but Katai had managed to keep her alive. She knew if he ever learned that Miri was trying to escape, the punishment would be unimaginable.

She had tried her best to keep Miri safe and comfortable in her mother's absence. And though Miri did not see things that way, Katai had found a sense of purpose in her protection of the girl. Now, it was all crashing down around her, and Katai was desperate to fix it before the Pit Fiend returned.

She shoved open the front doors of the keep, growling at the guards as they eyed her suspiciously. None dared to block her path, however, and she darted out across the bridge. Below her, the flames of the Hellfire Pit raged, teeming with the souls of devils and demons that Carnifax had punished in the past. One did not die when thrown in there; instead, their body was slowly mutated and warped by the fires. That was where Miri's brothers had gone when they failed to please the Pit Fiend. And that was where they remained to this day, writhing and shrieking as they became something worse with the passage of time.

She focused on the wastelands ahead, forcing herself to ignore the agonized screams of those trapped in the Pit. If she failed today, her own fate would be so very much worse than theirs... And Miri? Miri would be lucky to survive at all. Carnifax did not value her enough to warrant throwing her into the fire. She would be torn apart...

As she stepped onto the wastes, Katai spread her wings and took to the blackened sky. A land of sharp iron and jagged stone stretched out below her, inhospitable and cruel. Those who dared to run into that barren landscape rarely made it far, as minions of Carnifax patrolled the territory and mercilessly hunted down all who attempted to flee. Her sharp eyes scanned around for any sign of her charge and she sniffed at the air, desperate to find her before anyone else could.

There! Very faint beneath the smell of sulfur, she caught Miri's scent. The girl had made it to the very edge of Carnifax's territory, near the barrier the Pit Fiend had constructed to keep everything out. Only he could open it, which meant Miri had come to the end of the road. Katai veered around and chased after her, opening the mental link that bound them together and allowing her frustration to go ahead of her.

"Zhamiri! What do you think you are doing?!"

Immediately, she found herself bombarded by everything the girl was thinking and feeling. Fear of what was to come when Katai caught up with her. Desperation to escape from Carnifax after so long under his control. Hatred for the Blackstone Keep that had held her prisoner. And overpowering everything; hope. It was an emotion Katai did not understand, and it staggered her in its intensity. Miri actually believed she had found a way out! But that *couldn't* be possible! Could it...?

Katai pressed on, urging her wings to carry her faster. Soon, she caught sight of her charge in the distance, pacing like a caged animal on the very edge of the barrier. Miri's dark skin glowed red in a flash of crimson lightning. Her wings, still battered from her last meeting with Carnifax, trembled behind her. And she looked back at Katai with a panicked expression.

"There is nowhere to go, Child!" Katai sent to her with a wave of anger. *"Come back with me before we're caught out here!"*

But Miri only shook her head in defiance. Katai hissed angrily. If they made it out of this in one piece, she was going to tan the girl's hide!

Then, beyond all belief, a hole opened in Carnifax's barrier and a portal stretched wide before it. Miri spun to face it as Katai looked on in horror, nearly dropping out of the sky in her shock. A pale hand reached through, trying to take something from the girl. And through the mental link, Katai suddenly understood. Miri wasn't just trying to run; she was attempting to leave the Hells entirely. Someone was helping her from the Prime Material Plane!

"No!" she shrieked aloud. Coming in to land, she rushed forward and shoved Miri back with all of her strength as the girl locked hands with her would-be rescuer. Whatever the girl was giving them would act as a conduit to summon her. Katai *had* to get it back before they completed their spell!

"They cannot take you from me!"

Enraged, Katai broke the contact between Miri and her savior, then she snatched at the wrist of the one reaching through the portal. Yanking hard, she attempted to wrench him through the doorway onto her side, and her eyes fixed on the lock of crimson hair he clutched in one metal fist. Miri cried out for her to stop, even going so far as to strike at her, but Katai couldn't stop. She had to put an end to this and get Miri away before Carnifax noticed the breach in his defenses. Before she, herself, lost everything!

She glared into a pair of purple eyes as the startled elf on the other side pulled against her grip. He was strong, but not strong enough to free himself. She yanked again, nearly bringing him though the portal, and snarled into his pale face. He brought his free hand up to shove against her and Katai felt the chill of the metal in stark contrast to the heat of her surroundings.

"You will not have her!" she screeched. "I cannot fail him again!" She slashed at him, breathing in his scent and memorizing it. Should he possibly succeed in this endeavor, she intended to hunt him across the planes and rip him limb from limb!

But his scent was not the only one she picked up. Katai's gaze flicked past the elf, taking in the room he stood in with a sudden sense of dread. A grand summoning circle was set up across the chamber. Gathered around it were three others; two older humans that she did not know, and one very familiar Deep elf girl that she had thought never to see again. Instantly, Katai felt her stomach drop.

Gzifa...

She was in poor shape. Her face was drawn and gaunt, filled with desperation. She mouthed Katai's name and her body trembled weakly. And for a moment, Katai was tempted to stop fighting. A deep longing filled her; a desire to release the elf male and to beg to be brought along in the summoning. If she could be rejoined with Gzifa, then both she and Miri would be safe! But before she could act, everything began to happen very quickly.

The elf before her extended his metal hand, warping and stretching it across the room to the circle. Then he spun back and slashed at her with it as it morphed into the shape of a blade. Katai shrieked, tightening her grip on him and pulling him closer to keep him from escaping. He lost his footing momentarily and his eyes narrowed in determination. Then he sucked in a breath and shut the portal on his own arm.

Thrown backward by her own strength, Katai tumbled away in a spray of blood, her grasp still tight on the twitching, severed limb. Behind her, Miri gasped in shock. Then a pale glow began to emanate around the girl. The spell was beginning. Katai scrambled to face her, dropping the arm and reaching out for her.

"Zhamiri, wait!" she cried desperately.

Then a new energy was falling over the wastelands, heavy and oppressive. Both Katai and Miri dropped to their knees as Carnifax turned his attention toward the hole in his defenses. For the moment, his eyes were fixed on those beyond the barrier; fixed on Gzifa, who had escaped him so long ago... But Katai knew it was only a matter of time before he looked their way as well. And once that happened, any chance of escape would go up in flames. If they were lucky, she and Miri would both be thrown into the Pit, and everything that made them who they were would be burned away. If they were lucky...

The call rang out from across the Planes, *"Zhamiri!"* It was Gzifa's voice, reaching out to summon her daughter to her side.

Katai felt her heart shatter at the familiar tone, so filled with pain and fear, and she knew that there was only one option left.

She met Miri's frightened eyes and knew the girl's chances were dwindling. And in that moment, she made a decision that was entirely selfless. She let go of her claim to her charge.

As she had done only once before, with Gzifa as the girl strove for one viable pregnancy, Katai offered her own energy to the magic in the air. The spell surrounding Miri activated, spurred into motion by Katai's contribution. The girl vanished in a flash of light, and within moments Katai's connection to her was severed entirely.

Left alone to face Carnifax's power, Katai stared down at the golden manacles on her wrists. They were cold and silent, leaving her mind empty, save for her own thoughts, for the first time in centuries. Miri was gone, the link was broken. And in that quiet, Katai felt something break within her.

She tilted her head back and screamed at the turmoil that raged inside her. It was all too much! Too many emotions to process or to accept.

Fury that a group of mortals could get the better of her.

Terror at the thought of what Carnifax would do to her now.

Shame at having failed yet again, though she knew it was out of her control.

And beyond all else, grief for the broken connection. For what she had lost... That last shocked her with its strength, and she fell into silent sobs as the despair washed over her.

Katai was surprised by how deeply she cared for both Miri and Gzifa. She was a succubus, and was thus more accustomed to creating desire in others. But this was something different. Something deeper. It was an emotion she could not comprehend, though she knew it to be akin to what Gzifa felt for Miri. And she realized that it was love...

Despite the terrible gravity of the situation she was now trapped in, Katai found she could not be angry with either Gzifa or Miri. Rather, she discovered a well of relief that the half-demon girl had managed to escape at last, and even more that Gzifa was still alive out there in the Mortal Realm. They were reunited. They were safe...

And oh, how Katai longed to join them...

But she knew that was impossible, and she recognized the path her life was taking would lead her in another direction entirely.

Carnifax was coming. He would be arriving sooner than she liked, his energy growing like a storm cloud around her. Composing herself slowly, Katai focused her attention on him. The barrier was resealing itself, and he was coming home to inspect and to punish. By the sheer rage that was choking her, Katai knew he was already aware of what had occurred in his absence, even if he hadn't noticed the culprit yet. But Katai, resigned to her fate, resisted the urge to try to run. There would be no escape this time, no talking herself out of trouble, and she would likely not survive the Pit Fiend's wrath. But there was work to be done, and she could still act to ensure that Carnifax did not follow Miri's trail back to Gzifa...

Turning to regard the elf's severed arm, she took a breath and let go of her thoughts of revenge. She cast her first spell. The limb disintegrated, scattering away across the wastelands. Once it was gone, Katai cast again, this time focusing on the place where the portal had opened. Shining glyphs flashed in the air and faded out, taking with them all traces of the hole and the people who had caused it. All that would be left was her magic, drowning out all else. But even that wouldn't be enough.

Katai looked down at her golden manacles and sighed. She couldn't afford to have Carnifax digging through her mind for the truth or all would be lost. Miri had to simply disappear as Gzifa had. So there was nothing else for it. But at least she wouldn't feel anything after... That alone came as a relief to her.

Katai's final spell was one she had learned in the days of her youth and never had any real use for. It was originally designed by the first dwarves of Lapus, to serve as a burial ceremony. Only a mortal of pure heart would be able to reverse it, which made it the perfect defense against Carnifax. Katai could hope that she would one day be free, but she doubted that would ever come to pass. No one would even know what she had done...

The golden manacles sank into her wrists, becoming one with her flesh. Gradually, the metal began to spread outward, overtaking her body inch by inch. With it came a stiffening of her limbs, which the succubus did not try to fight. Rather, she welcomed the deep stillness that was filling her. She lifted her hands toward the inky sky, looking upward as her thoughts receded. Soon, she would be completely encased, consumed, and it would all be over.

Katai's final thoughts as she shrank away were warm and comforting. She was with Gzifa and Miri again in their shared chamber, cuddled together in sleep, and that was where she intended to stay. She knew she had done all she could to protect the drow woman and their shared daughter. And while she was content in the knowledge that they were safe, she prayed to whatever deity had taken Gzifa from her in the first place that there was a future out there where she might see them both again. Then even that was gone, and her mind fell into the blissful oblivion of endless slumber.

By the time Carnifax made it to that part of the wastelands, Katai was gone. All that was left of her was a small golden statuette of a beautiful elven woman, her arms raised in praise and supplication...

RACHAEL KNIGHT

The Realm of the Gods

A chime sounded overhead, drawing Jack's attention away from his work. Looking over to the door, he could see the green gem over the frame glowing brightly. That was the signal from the bar, which meant Rus was looking for him. And as he generally handled things well enough on his own, that could only mean it was something important.

With a sigh, Jack set down his quill and gathered together his notes. "I suppose cataloging will have to wait," he murmured under his breath. Then he picked up a darkened and cracked gemstone he had been recording and took it to the back wall of the little chamber. There, he placed it on an open shelf, labeled *CURSED*, and stepped back to admire his ever-growing collection of magic items. A real lucky rabbit's foot. A golden cage with a mechanical cricket inside. A silver horseshoe. And so many other things he had gathered over the years.

The chime sounded again and Jack spun about with a groan. "All right, all right," he groused. "I'm coming..."

It wasn't like Rus to be impatient, so he picked up the pace as he made his way through the passage and secret doorway from his hidden chamber. It let him out in the cellar, where he took the stairs two at a time to reach the exit just behind the bar.

Fortune's Folly was crowded as ever, packed to the brim with people celebrating one of Menzo's many holidays. Those at the bar saluted Jack as they caught sight of him, toasting the second owner of the establishment with drunken vigor. Somewhere in the large front room, a bard was performing, and Jack caught enough of the lyrics to recognize one of his own adventures.

Rus turned his way immediately, a frown on his face. "Were you expecting someone tonight?" he asked without preamble as he piled mugs onto a tray for one of the serving girls.

Jack shook his head slowly. "I don't think so," he said with a glance around. "Who's asking for me?"

"The young woman by the fireplace," Rus replied. "She says she has an appointment with you."

"Did you get her name?"

Rus snorted. “Do you see this place? I hardly have time to fill an order before a dozen more are thrown at me. I’m telling you, it’s time to hire more people to help out in here. Hells, hire this girl! Maybe that’s why she’s here.”

Then he was pulled back to the patrons, hurrying about the bar with practiced ease despite his complaints. Jack let him go, quietly agreeing that perhaps it was time to get another server in the joint... If this was how Fortune's Folly was starting to look on a regular basis, there was no way Rus could continue to run it on his own.

He worked his way slowly through the crowd, greeting the regulars who called out to him. And as he approached the fireplace, he finally caught sight of the woman who was asking for him. Right away, Jack was certain he had never seen the woman before, which made this ‘appointment’ all the more suspect. Jack took care not to show his discomfort with the situation, however, as he moved into the woman’s field of view.

“Rus said you were looking for me?” he said in his coolest tone.

The woman’s face split into a wide smile. “Jack Tindal!” she said warmly. “And right on time, too! Please, sit.”

Jack was used to people knowing him by this point. His work to free the city from the influence of the Muses had done wonders for his reputation. But there was a familiarity to the stranger’s tone that made him wonder. “I’m sorry, but do we know each other?”

“Not officially, no,” the woman replied. “But I am hoping to amend that today.” She motioned to the seat across from her, inviting Jack to join her. “I have need of your assistance with a matter of... rather grave importance.”

“And what matter would that be?”

The woman glanced around. “It isn’t something to discuss openly.”

Jack crossed his arms over his chest and scoffed. “Look, Lady, *you* asked to see *me*. If you can’t just get to the point, I’ll take my leave. I already have a lot on my plate and I don’t need to be jerked around by your troubles as well." He turned to walk away.

"Trust me; you'll *want* to be a part of this, Jack!" the woman called out, and there was no desperation in her voice. Only calm confidence.

Jack turned back, studying the stranger again. "Why?"

The woman reached into her jerkin, pulling out a small coin purse. Placing three gold pieces on the table, she slid them toward Jack. "I will pay for a room right now if you will agree to discuss this matter with me in private. We'll only need a few moments, but I am happy to cover the cost of the room for a night anyway. All you have to do is listen, then you can tell me what you feel like doing with the information I give you. Sound fair?"

Jack sighed. The woman was offering far more than the room was worth for a night. "Fine," he said after a moment. "We'll go upstairs, then, and I'll hear you out. But I'm not making any promises here."

He started for the upper landing, the beaming stranger falling into step beside him. "You won't regret this, Jack," the woman told him.

"I think I'll be the judge of that," Jack retorted. He glanced over as they started up the stairs. "What did you say your name was?"

"I didn't," the woman said with a soft giggle. "But you can refer to me as Chloe."

"Any last name to go with that?"

Chloe paused as they reached the landing, her expression genuinely confused. "Do you really think I need one? I hadn't considered it..."

Jack couldn't think of a response to that. He pushed ahead of the stranger to open the door of one of their vacant rooms. As he turned the knob, he glanced back at Chloe. The woman seemed honest enough, but she was an odd one, and Jack was only growing more curious by the second. Then they were stepping through the doorway and the familiarity of Fortune's Folly vanished between one step and the next...

* * *

It was a library, both eerily familiar and absolutely alien in its design. For a brief moment, Jack was certain that he had somehow returned to the Grand Library at the heart of the Labyrinth. But no. This place was exponentially larger, seeming to stretch on endlessly in every direction, and the bookcases towered overhead, taller than any of the buildings in Menzo.

The sounds of the bar at Fortune's Folly vanished with the snap of the door closing. Jack spun around just in time to watch the door vanish, leaving yet another infinite row of shelves behind them. And far down that row, Jack could see an open space, taken up by a round table and crowded with other people.

"What... what is all this?" Jack asked once he remembered how to speak.

Chloe looked around as if it were obvious. "My realm. What else would it be?"

Jack blinked. "Your realm," he repeated slowly. "Does that make you some sort of goddess?"

"Not just any goddess, Jack Tindal," a new voice answered him as one of the figures at the table broke away to approach them. "You are in the presence of the Elder Gods, Child; mind how you speak."

Jack studied the newcomer with his mouth dropping open. "But... I know you," he said. "You're..." But he couldn't bring himself to say the name aloud.

He was greatly changed from the figure Jack knew, and yet there was no denying his identity. His robes were inky black, adorned with red and gold. The crown atop his head was of living vines and flowers, locked in a constant state of growth and decay. Images of dragons, the tattoos of his intensive martial training, danced and flowed across his skin.

There was an aura of power around him that Jack had never felt before. It was ancient and infinite, contained within him and permeating the air around him with every move he made. This was certainly not the same man he had encountered during him trials against the Muses. But there was no mistaking him; he was just older and by far more powerful than Jack had ever seen him, which was saying something when he considered the great warrior he knew...

"You're saying *you're* an Elder God, too?" Jack shook his head. "How in the Hells is that possible?"

The figure didn't bother to answer the question. He regarded Jack in silence for a moment, then sighed. "Such disrespect...," he muttered.

"It's all right, Cadenza," Chloe cut in, leaning into him and pressing a hand to his heart. "He's here to help us, aren't you, Jack?"

"A matter I still don't think is entirely necessary," the one called Cadenza retorted. "We have other options."

"But none are as good as him," Chloe told him with a knowing smile.

Jack cleared his throat. "Sorry... But I still don't know what exactly I'm supposed to be helping you with." He glanced around at the library and shook his head. "It isn't like you're giving me much *choice* in helping, but I'd at least like to understand what I'm agreeing to..."

"And if you can't understand it, what then?" Cadenza asked sharply. "You'll refuse?"

Jack scoffed. "Refuse the Elder Gods? I'm not stupid enough for that." He shook his head again, more vigorously. "I just want to know what I'm signing up for. So long as *you* understand the process behind my involvement, I'll take that as good enough."

Chloe clapped her hands excitedly, her smile wide. "Wonderful!" she exclaimed. Then she took hold of Jack's arm and led him toward the table. "Come meet the others and we'll explain everything!"

*   *   *

The area surrounding the table was clear of everything save

a series of podiums, which were evenly spaced around it. Jack counted them as he stepped into the circle. Five; and each one held an open book, covered in scrawling runes that Jack could not read. The strange words seemed to move on the page, and the more he tried to focus on them, the more he found a headache building behind his eyes. Looking away, he turned his attention to the table, and to the four figures who waited there.

Two, he recognized instantly. Gzifa was a regular at Fortune's Folly, and she had brought her friend Dreamwalker along on more than one occasion. But the others were unknown to him. One was a fierce-looking human woman, a warrior from what Jack could see, and the other was a Deep elf with a face so similar to Dreamwalker's that it could only be his brother. As he approached, they all glanced his way.

Jack fixed Gzifa with a wide smile. "Well, if it isn't the Lady of Frost! Fancy seeing you here!"

Gzifa frowned. "Excuse me…?" she responded in obvious confusion. She glanced to the human woman, who shrugged, then looked back to Jack. "I'm sorry, have we met?"

That was not the reply Jack expected. His smile fading, he chuckled nervously. "What are you talking about? You came in for a drink just two days ago!"

"I did?" Gzifa only sounded more confused.

Jack nodded vigorously. "Yeah… Fire wine at the Winter Solstice Festival? You even mentioned you'd be seeing me soon…" Jack paused, considering the claim. "That suddenly makes much more sense, now that I've said it out loud. You must have known I'd be called here, too."

Gzifa slowly shook her head. "I really think you have the wrong person…," she said softly. "I've never seen you before in my life."

"...What…?" At a loss, Jack turned to look at Dreamwalker. "*You* still remember me, at least, right?" he asked hopefully. "Tell me you haven't both gone crazy."

He appeared startled to be singled out next, but Dreamwalker didn't immediately answer. He studied Jack carefully and he felt the familiar tickle as the psionicist's mind brushed his own. Then Dreamwalker drew back and took a breath. "I'm sure I've never met you... But I'm also certain you believe you know us," he said cryptically. Tilting his head slightly, he asked, "Where do you come from?"

Chloe let out a giggle. "Not *where*," she interjected.

At her side, Cadenza nodded. "*When*," he corrected smoothly. He glanced to Gzifa. "Though he is a stranger to you now, Jack will be well-known to you in your future."

"My future?" Gzifa shook her head. "So, this is more of your work, then?"

"Of a sort," Cadenza said nonchalantly. He gestured to the podiums surrounding them. "As you can see, each of your books is open to a certain page-"

"*Our* books?" Jack interrupted.

Cadenza sighed. "Yes. Every living being in creation has their own story recorded in the Scribe's Library. These books detail every second of your lives. Your actions, your choices, and your innermost thoughts. Some, like yours, Jack, are exceptionally long. Others, Like Riley's, Gzifa's, Theofred's, and Eglandir's have the possibility of being infinite."

"You're saying they outclass immortality?" Jack asked in surprise.

"*You* can still die, Jack Tindal," Cadenza told him firmly. "So while yours certainly has infinite *potential*, your story can also come to an end."

"But... theirs can't...?" It seemed to confuse Gzifa and the others just as much as it confounded Jack. He scowled, trying to wrap his head around a concept of life beyond immortality.

Chloe spoke up, breaking the silence. "What matters right now is that I chose to pull Jack from further along in his timeline than the rest of you. This means he has memories of you, while none of you have yet to officially meet him."

"Isn't that a bit risky?" the one who looked like Dreamwalker asked. Jack figured he had to be Eglandir. "He can tell us things about our future, though I doubt anything he says will compare to what's in these books..."

"It can be dangerous, yes," Cadenza agreed with another sigh, "but I suppose that is where I come in. Generally, I wouldn't allow you to encounter each other early. But as this is a special occasion, I can make an exception and bend the rules of Time a bit. We've called you all here to accomplish what we cannot, or rather should not, do on our own."

Jack didn't like the sound of that, though he was certain he caught a look of disdain on Cadenza's face. Did he not believe his own words? "And what is it, exactly, that you need us to do?" he dared ask.

"Exactly what you have been working toward for years," Chloe told him with an encouraging smile. "You know. The adventure you and your companions went on to find the Book of Fiction? And more specifically, what you used it for?"

Jack glanced to the book Cadenza had pointed out as his. "So you know about that, too, huh?"

Chloe laughed. "I know about everything. Besides, do you really think you can enter the Library of the Labyrinth and not catch my eye? That place is only an extension of this realm." She nodded with absolute certainty. "I know all about you and your abilities, Jack, as well as what you accomplished there by writing in the Book *twice*. A feat that no one else has ever managed. And now, I'm giving you the opportunity to use what you gained."

* * *

The table they stood around was composed of crystal and shone with an inner light. Up close, an image could be seen on its surface; a planet... an entire world that Jack did not recognize. Great chunks of rock surrounded the space around it, slowly being drawn in by the planet's gravity. And as Jack watched, some began to ignite in the atmosphere. So much debris... That couldn't have happened by accident. No; this was intentional destruction on a massive scale...

Cadenza took a breath. "To get you up to speed with

everything, I will explain what you're looking at."

"No need," Jack said softly. "I recognize an attack when I see one. What world is this?"

"My own creation," Cadenza told him stiffly. "Once green and fertile, bursting with life, you know it in your own day as a desolate world; lost because of an act of extreme rage and hatred."

Jack shook his head. There was only one dead planet that he knew of, Veronus, and this place was nothing like it. To know what it looked like before only made him sad to consider what it was doomed to become.

"Who would do this?" he asked. "And what about the people who live there?"

"That is exactly why we are all gathered here," Chloe said gently. "The people of Veronus have been preserved, but they cannot remain in my realm indefinitely. If we wish to truly save them, we must provide them with a new home."

"But... you're the Elder Gods, right?" Jack pressed. "Can't you just... I don't know... *undo* the damage and send the people home?"

Cadenza answered with limitless patience, his tone solemn. "We could, but we won't. You already know what Veronus will be like. This is where that existence begins. This is the way the planet dies, and much depends on this moment in time. We should not alter that... But that does not mean that my people have to die along with it..."

Jack knew better than to argue. "All right," he agreed. "So where do I come in?"

"Your part to play is involved in re-homing our refugees," Chloe told him. She waved a hand and the image on the table switched to a view of another world; this one very familiar. "We've already sent the dragons to Lapus," Chloe explained, indicating the planet. "But this world is still in its infancy. I would rather not drop another entire civilization of strangers on the elves and dwarves that are building their lives there. But that only leaves us one other option..."

The table changed again and Jack was suddenly gazing

down at his own home world, Nerus. But something was wrong... Parts of the land had turned dark. Jack felt his stomach drop as a deep dread swept over him. The planet itself was sick.

"What era are we looking at?" he demanded softly.

Chloe gave him a knowing look. "The Age of Blight," she replied. "I'm sure you've heard of it."

Of course Jack had heard of it. The Age of Blight had a reputation as one of the darkest times in Nerus' history. "So let me get this straight... You want to dump a bunch of refugees in the middle of the Wars of Dissonance? The longest and bloodiest conflict this world has ever known? The people already on the planet are at each others' throats! Elven and human lives wiped out by the thousands! And it will be centuries before the land is healed."

"Like I said," Chloe sighed, "we don't have much choice. These people must have a new world. And I must do something to make things right before we can move them." She shook her head. "In many ways, the chaos down there is on me. If I had been more understanding and patient with Të, perhaps our personal conflicts wouldn't have leaked down onto the planet..."

Të was a name Jack had only heard once, in an ancient history text from Nerus. He recognized it as the name of another supposed god of the old world. "Wait, wait. You're saying you had a quarrel upstairs and *that* caused the blight?"

"Not directly," the Elder Goddess said ashamedly. "But what we did was enough to drive the mortals to the decisions that brought about this disaster... And now, something must be done to make amends."

"And what do you propose we do, then?" Jack demanded.

"Haven't you guessed?" Cadenza asked. "It's time for Nerus' Guardians to appear."

"We need to summon them here, now," Chloe added with a smile returning to her face.

"But what does that accomplish?" Gzifa blurted out, finally breaking her long silence. "What can they do that we can't?"

Chloe chuckled. She looked around at the others then shook

her head. “Forgive me,” she told them. “I keep forgetting that you haven’t learned this yet...” She motioned to Jack. “Would you mind showing our friends a little of what you’re capable of?”

Smirking, Jack obliged. He met Gzifa’s gaze and initiated the shift. His skin became inky black and leathery wings sprouted from his back. He felt fangs grow in his mouth and horns sprout from his forehead. And his male form became delicate and feminine. As the change was completed, he flipped crimson hair off his face and winked. Gzifa’s expression warped with confused longing.

“Miri,” she breathed. “You know my daughter?”

Jack nodded. “I’ve met her more than once,” he confirmed in Miri’s voice. He glanced to Dreamwalker. “And I know your kids, too.”

“Oh, really?” Dreamwalker mused, his eyes going wide. “I wasn’t aware I could have children...”

“It’s probably best not to pursue that line of thought,” Cadenza warned sternly. “It can be dangerous to know too much about your own future.” He gestured to Jack to drop the disguise. “Let’s get back on topic, shall we?”

“Right,” Chloe agreed. “The Guardians, like Jack here, are a separate race entirely. They are shape shifters; highly magical beings, and practically immortal. They are expert warriors, who hold the kind of celestial power that is necessary to cleanse the corruption from Nerus. And it is nearly time for them to emerge on the planet to begin their work.”

“Okay...,” Gzifa said slowly, still frowning. “But you’re talking about calling together the ones that already exist. How does summoning future generations work for us?”

“That is, once again, where *I* come in,” Cadenza responded coolly. “With a little cooperation from Jack, and quite a hefty bit of Time and Life magics from me, we should be able to recreate their original template.”

Gzifa scoffed. “Recreate... a race of people?”

Cadenza nodded. “It sounds strange, I know,” he conceded, “but we need the Guardians on Nerus, now, and there is no other way to go about this."

The one known as Eglandir spoke up. "So we *use* them to *make* them?"

Jack shrugged. "I mean, that works for me. As long as you can make it work, I already said I don't need to understand it."

Gzifa nodded. "I suppose that's true," she said reluctantly. "But I'm still curious... If we rewrite history and make it so the Guardians are created from themselves, then what are we replacing? What created them in the first place?"

Cadenza sighed heavily. "The one who was supposed to create them just lost his existence on Veronus," he explained quietly. The answer seemed to make sense to the others, who fell silent and somber almost instantly. Jack didn't ask further; noting the stiff way Cadenza clenched his jaw, he figured it was best not to interrupt him. "Now, we must make up for his loss by ensuring these people are still made. And that, my friends, is what we call a major paradox, which is why we need to do this very carefully. Because one mistake could lead to a level of destruction that makes Veronus look like child's play."

"That's encouraging...," Eglandir and Jack said in unison.

* * *

Those who were guests to the library were asked very politely to remain close to the table as Chloe went about making space for all of them to work. The library shifted and moved according to the Elder Goddess' whims, the shelves sliding away to clear the floor. And for the first time, Jack could see in its entirety the massive mural that stretched across the domed ceiling high overhead. The image was that of a great two-headed dragon, suspended amid a sea of stars. In its claws, it held the sun, and its twin jaws were stretched wide in cries of triumph. Even from far away, Jack was awed by the detail of the painting. It seemed so lifelike... as if it could turn and look back at him at any moment. And Jack found he couldn't take his eyes off of it until his attention was forcibly pulled back to the task at hand.

"We're ready for you now, Jack." When had Chloe returned to the table?

Jack shook himself and took a breath. "Nothing to it," he said with more confidence than he felt.

Jack was what was known as a Paragon. Even beyond the powers of the Guardians, he possessed something unique within the world. For he carried within him the potential to turn his will into a reality, to do anything he set his mind to. With a thought, he could copy spells or accomplish feats that he had only ever seen. But the power was not guaranteed to work. Rather, it depended solely on luck whether he could achieve his goals or not. But that was the whole point of what he had written into the Book of Fiction; to make that potential a little more concrete...

He had not yet had a chance to test the improvements to the power as he had written it out for himself within the Labyrinth. He had no idea if it would actually work the way he planned. So as he stepped out into the open space, an area larger than some arenas he had attended, he prayed that the magic would do its job...

"It will work," Chloe called out, and Jack flinched as she read his mind. But he did not slow to a stop until he was directly beneath the dragon mural.

Steadying himself one last time, Jack shook away his nerves and reached out to his sides. On his command, the power rose up around him. Jack never faltered as he felt the familiar weight settle into place, like a blanket wrapping close about his body. He knew without a doubt that his wish had been granted by the Book. And right away, he felt that first quiver of something new and familiar; excitement.

"Nothing to it," he repeated with more vigor. He focused his will upon the outcome he desired; to call his people to his location. Then he activated the magic.

Golden-white runes ignited in the air around him. Jack took a deep breath, drawing the magic to him with a thought. Then he swung his hands in, driving them together in a clap of sound and a blast of light. Power surged around Jack, strong enough to steal his breath, and he recognized it instantly. Even before his vision returned, he knew the magic had worked because he could sense them. All of them...

The massive chamber was suddenly filled with thousands of voices, all clamoring to be heard. Shouts of surprise and fear, cries of shock, questions... It all came together in a great wall of sound, in which no one voice could be distinguished from the rest.

Jack blinked spots from his eyes, staring around with growing awe. These were the Guardians in their entirety: past, present, and future generations; including all those who had died and all those yet to be born. Jack saw so many faces he knew and had lost, and so many more that he couldn't recognize. More Guardians that he had ever dreamed of seeing in a single place. All of the Families, gathered together in a way that never happened before, and never would again. And it filled Jack with a fierce pride and joy.

But of course, Jack also anticipated that not all who were brought to the library would be so pleased with such a turn of events. There were hundred of Outcasts, traitors to their Families, scattered throughout the crowd. Their eyes shone with that ominous ring of stars, and the rest of the Guardians were quick to turn on these individuals, their most-hated rivals. New cries arose from the crowd, accusatory, threatening, and many reached for their magic as the tension climbed. But no magic came to their call, and those who resorted to physical violence found they were unable to harm their targets.

Jack sighed as the chaos continued to grow. These people were confused, angry, frightened, and on edge. The magic of Chloe's realm would prevent them from hurting each other, but that would do little to calm them down. He needed to take charge of the situation, force them to listen, if they ever hoped to get to work on the Elder Gods' plans.

A single thought to his magic sent a siren call out over the crowd. It echoed through the shelves, distorting and growing louder over time.

"QUIET!" he roared over the din of voices, and as he did so,

a pillar of fire rose up around him. The flames whipped his hair about but did not touch him. He embraced the heat, noting that every eye was now turned his way. And as he released the flames, the roar of the fire died away to absolute silence.

Jack smirked with satisfaction as he noted the shock and wonder on the faces around him. He cleared his throat, standing tall.

"Now that I have your attention," he said brightly, "let's talk."

* * *

Once everyone understood what was being asked of them, each was offered a choice: Any who had no interest in participating in the Elder Gods' spell could return to wherever- and wherever- they originally came from. Jack expected at least a few to take this chance to leave, but his people surprised him. It seemed both the Outcasts and the House members were more than willing to take part, in the hopes of passing their own wills and intents to the new race. Not a single Guardian asked to leave early.

Thus the work began. One by one, the Guardians stepped forward to impart a piece of themselves into a massive crystal, which Chloe brought into being at the heart of the room. The crystal grew steadily brighter with each new addition of life energy placed within it. And ever so slowly, those already finished with their part began to disappear.

Jack moved among them with wonder and a bittersweet joy. He spoke to friends and family who were lost to him in his own time, and embraced his brothers and sisters one last time. He reveled in the moment, throwing himself into conversations with reckless abandon, because he knew it couldn't last forever. In his era, there were so few Guardians left, and many of the smiling faces around him would soon be dead and gone once more. And Jack intended to cherish what little time he had with his kin before that time ran out.

There was plenty of talk of reparations going around. Jack overheard several discussions involving Guardians meeting together in their own times to fix the rifts in their Families. But Jack knew that none of them would even remember being here once they were sent home. No; that honor would go solely to the bearer of the magic that summoned them. So Jack made a mental note to uphold their plans on his own. He wasn't even sure how he would manage it, but the 'how' hardly mattered, and he intended to unite his people in earnest once more, at whatever cost...

Little by little, the library cleared, and as it did, the tall shelves crept back in to fill the space. Sooner than Jack liked, the last of his kin were gone and the room felt empty and cold. He stood beside the great crystal, now too bright to look at directly, and felt some of the excitement fading. The crystal emanated a familiar and comforting energy, but it was a pale comparison to the real deal, and Jack mourned the loss.

A hand alighted on his shoulder, drawing him back from heavy thoughts. Chloe smiled warmly. "You've done well," she said with pride. "You're welcome to go home now, if that is what you would like."

Jack shook his head. "If it's all the same to you, I'd rather stay and see the rest of this play out."

Chloe's eyes shone with understanding. "Very well," she conceded. "Go and join the others. You can remain in the library until the task is complete, but I really must insist you leave as soon as we're finished. Even you, with your unique abilities, should not linger in this realm for longer than necessary."

Jack returned to the table with new musings to occupy his mind. What manner of effects could possibly happen if he stayed in the library too long? And were they necessarily bad effects? This was the realm of the Elder Gods, after all. Surely it couldn't be something deadly? And if it was, what could it do to him? But these were questions he never got the chance to voice, as Chloe and Cadenza began to work on the next step of their plans.

The pair stood shoulder to shoulder before the blinding crystal. Chloe snapped her fingers and a large tome dropped into her open hand. Jack recognized the Book of Fiction, instantly. Turning to a blank page, she produced a quill, seemingly from nowhere, and began to write. At her side, Cadenza started to chant and the crystal thrummed in time with the rhythm of his spell. Then the light began to swirl and move, reaching out from its prison in hundreds of glowing tendrils. Where it touched the ground, it solidified and grew, until hundreds of humanoid forms could be seen within the light.

The crystal dimmed, its stored energy now evenly dispersed among the new-made bodies. For a moment, the beings of light pulsed and flickered, then they grew solid. Jack released a breath he hadn't realized he was holding.

"It will take a few moments for our new friends to awaken fully," Chloe announced as Cadenza's spell came to a close. "Imparting the knowledge of their purpose requires some time." The Elder Goddess scribbled a few last details into her book, then shut it with a snap. "Feel free to take a closer look if you want to."

Jack stepped up to one of the figures and blinked in surprise. They were much larger than him, taller and broader across the shoulders, and there were no real discerning features to any of them. No way to tell their House or bloodline. And as he gazed into its glassy blue eyes, Jack noted that even the symbol that should have been in the irises was something new; a figure eight, turned on its side.

"What is this?" Jack asked softly.

"Your peoples' true form," Chloe told him in a matter-of-fact tone. "The first generation were so much more than you realize, and their unique quality is marked with my own sign as a result."

"And what does it mean?"

Cadenza answered this time. "It means eternity. It means life and creation. It means *everything*, marking a balance in all things."

"That is the duty you are made for; maintaining the natural order." Chloe shrugged. "Of course, such a purpose will change over time, and so will the limits of the Guardians' powers..."

"But why would we change?" Jack pressed. "This looks much stronger than what I know... Why would we ever shift away from it?"

"That is the nature of Life," Cadenza responded simply. "Everything evolves based upon necessity. So when the time comes that such power is no longer needed, it becomes something new."

"Be patient," Chloe advised. "You'll see it for yourself soon enough."

* * *

When the new-made Guardians were fully awake, Cadenza took the time to explain their orders to them. But it was as if no explanation was really needed. These people seemed to know their mission on a spiritual level; an instinct they could not ignore. So when a portal was opened onto Nerus, they filed through without a single word of argument, appearing almost eager to step in and quell the chaos of their new world. And Gzifa and her companions went along with them, leaving Jack alone with the Elder Gods to watch events play out through the images displayed in the table.

He looked on with genuine interest as they arrived on the planet in the midst of a great battle. And there, he witnessed at last the true power of his people. There were no divisions of Families or House magic. Instead, all could access whatever magics they required in the moment: Elemental, psychic, temporal, healing... It all came from a shared pool, and Jack discovered a new emotion as he watched the Wars of Dissonance come to an end: Jealousy. He wanted a chance to wield such power! And it surprised him how great that desire was.

Time passed differently between the realm of mortals and the realm of the Elder Gods. In a matter of minutes, the battle was over and cleanup began. Mutated versions of the elves were destroyed. Monstrous animals were slain or driven away to save human cities. Elven territories were cleansed of the remains of the

Blight which afflicted them. And little by little, Nerus was restored to a peaceful existence.

Then came the first major shift in the aftermath of the Wars: the world was divided up. To the north of the great mountain range that split the land, the elves laid claim to the forest. This was their ancestral home, and though peace had been restored between the races, they were ready to close it off to their neighbors permanently. And to the south of the mountains, mankind laid claim to everything else.

The time had come at last for the Guardians to change as well. Gzifa and her friends spent many years building a grand kingdom for the refugees from Veronus. In that time, most of the Guardians lived openly upon the land and worked as a singular unit to populate and prepare the kingdom for the new arrivals. But as the elves and humans separated, and the construction drew to a close, the Guardians needed to alter their own way of life to maintain their primary mission of upholding the balance.

"There they go," Chloe said with a smile. "The world has spread out, and now so must the Guardians. This is the moment where they first split into smaller factions. Some remain around the land of New Veron, others choose to live among the elves, and the rest will disperse among the human kingdoms. Now watch..."

Jack leaned closer, peering in on one of the groups with interest as decades slipped by in seconds. What would have gone unnoticed in the moment became clearly visible to his eyes. These Guardians grew smaller, more wiry with each new generation. The infinity symbol faded away, and eventually only one magic could be summoned. Jack noted with surprise that it was his own power, the magic of the berserker warriors. And as his Family star sign blossomed in their eyes, he at last recognized the start of his own House.

"With the fighting done, all of that incredible power was no longer needed," Chloe told him. "Each faction took a portion of the magic and mastered it. And in time, these factions became the Families. Does it make sense now?"

"Almost..." Jack shook his head. "I can understand why we

divided ourselves, and even why we divided the magic... But what happens to bring about the Outcast uprising?"

"Can't you guess?" Cadenza scoffed. "The younger generations eventually learn of that first divergence, of course. All it takes is one glimpse of the old magics for them to covet and crave it for themselves."

Chloe looked sad as she spoke up. "But the Outcasts could never reclaim that past strength. That time is passed, and what they gain instead is something without control or purpose. Their magic is unbound, even to them, and they claim it as superior to their own detriment."

Jack scowled. "When I left Nerus, the Outcasts were the greatest force on the planet. How does that amount to without control?"

"All who amplify their power in such a way are eventually consumed by it," Cadenza stated firmly. "Had you remained on Nerus, you would have witnessed the Outcasts' downfall at their own hands."

That gave Jack pause. "So there will come a time when that fight is over, too? My people will survive?"

Chloe laughed. "Oh no; it's already over for you. In your own time, I mean. Your people have survived, and they are rebuilding."

"Any chance you could show me that?" Jack breathed hopefully, though he knew what their answer would be.

"If you are meant to see that, you will do so along your own timeline," Cadenza told him sternly, "not from here." And that was the last either of the Elder Gods would speak of it. Jack didn't mind, however. He could be patient... And when he got back to Fortune's Folly, he would pay a visit to his home world. After all, with the Paragon power he possessed, there was no one who could stop him from going back to Nerus whenever he liked...

* * *

Jack was the only one at the table when the next doorway

opened and Gzifa's group returned from Nerus. They were one member fewer than when they left, but something told Jack that their human companion was anything but lost. And as Riley's book seemed to be growing thicker each time he glanced at it, that could only mean that the human was something more, something Jack had missed...

As for the others, they looked much the same physically. But Jack could see the centuries in their eyes; especially in Gzifa's, who he had visited with on multiple occasions. So much time spent in preparation for this exact moment. And at last, Nerus was ready.

"Where are they?" Gzifa asked. Jack didn't have to guess who she meant.

"Chloe said something about 'gathering the flock for their shepherds'," he said dully. "Cadenza went with her, and they've been gone for hours."

"They left you here alone?" Eglandir sounded surprised. He cracked a smile. "And you didn't think to take a peek at anything?"

Jack smirked back. "Of course I did," he told him, "but even I can't read the words in any of these books, so I gave up. Figured it was best just to wait until you got here."

Gzifa sighed. "Well, they can't have gone too far, right?"

"In an infinite library?" Jack snorted. "No, I doubt they could get far in a place like this."

Gzifa's eyes narrowed at the sarcastic tone. She opened her mouth to retort, but the sound of approaching footsteps quickly silenced her.

Chloe and Cadenza stepped back into view, the air surrounding them filled with small yellow crystals. There were thousands, hundreds of thousands, all swirling about and trailing after the pair in utter silence. Each gem glowed with an inner light, pulsing like a heartbeat.

"Are we all ready, then?" Chloe asked brightly.

"Everything is set up," Dreamwalker said with a respectful bow, "exactly as you instructed."

"Wonderful!" Chloe clapped softly and the crystals

gathered close together and soared away from her, toward Gzifa and the others. "Here are your charges. You should have just enough time to take them to their new home before they become free."

"Can I go?" Jack blurted. "Just for a little while? I feel useless here. I'd like to help if I can."

Cadenza studied him carefully, silently debating. After a moment, he sighed. "I suppose we can allow for a few minutes. You can accompany them for the drop-off, but that's it. The minute I call you back, you'd better return to the portal, understand? We can't have you accidentally altering this timeline. It's already strained enough with the changes we have made. Any more could drastically change the future."

Jack was nodding before he even finished speaking. "I got it, I got it." He grinned in anticipation. "How are we doing this?"

"The crystals will follow you through the portal on their own." Chloe held out another large book, offering it to Jack. "This is the manifest of every soul we saved. When you reach the planet, the crystals will open automatically and the book will begin crossing off names. When every name is crossed off, you know that everyone is accounted for."

"In the meantime," Cadenza chimed in imperiously, "stick to helping them gain their bearings and explaining the situation. No wandering. No touching anything. That goes for the rest of you, too." His sharp gaze turned to the others. "As some of you will not be remaining on Nerus after, we can't have you changing anything beyond this point. Once the transfer is complete, this will become a fixed point in the planet's history. Unchangeable."

Chloe clapped again. "I'm sure they'll be fine, Cadenza," she assured him happily. "And if not, you can always repair it."

She shooed them through the doorway, the crystals trailing behind them like fireflies. But Jack managed to catch the Elder God's response before he was pulled through the door.

"Yeah, but I would prefer to avoid that particular headache..."

* * *

The familiar warmth and sounds of Fortune's Folly washed over him as Jack followed Chloe back through a doorway and onto the upper landing of the bar. He breathed in the smell of home and sighed heavily.

"Just like that, it's done," he commented. "How long was I gone?"

Chloe shrugged. "No more than ten minutes," she said airily. "Rus will be surprised to see you back so soon, but not enough to worry. You can say you didn't like my proposition, and that will suffice for him. He won't ask questions."

"So I can't tell anyone about this?" Jack pouted.

"Not yet." Chloe smiled gently. "But you will be getting another visitor fairly soon. When they arrive, you can talk all you like to them. As for the rest of the world, it's best not to discuss such things. At least not until after you next see me."

"So I will be seeing you again..."

Chloe laughed. "Sooner than you'd expect," she confirmed. "Until then, I thank you for all you've done today. I am in your debt, and one day you will be rewarded for your service."

The Elder Goddess stepped backward into her library, her smile unwavering. With a final wave, she shut the door. And when Jack opened it again, he was left staring into an empty room of his bar. Not a thing was out of place and Chloe was long gone.

Jack sighed and turned back to the stairs, left with nothing but his memories to prove he had been gone at all. Rus caught his eye as he re-entered the bar.

"Not as intriguing as she made it sound, eh?"

"You could say that," Jack told him. "Need any help tonight?"

Rus shook his head. "Maybe in a bit, when the next rush starts. For now, you have another visitor."

Jack scowled. "I'm pretty popular tonight, aren't I?"

Rus chuckled. He slid a goblet and a bottle of Gloom-maiden

wine his way, and Jack immediately knew who had come calling. "She's at her usual table."

Jack snatched up the goods and spun away with a salute to Rus. Then he hurried through the busy common room to a far corner. There, he met Gzifa's knowing eyes and grinned wickedly.

"Fancy seeing you here!" he remarked for the second time that day.

This time, Gzifa laughed. She beckoned Jack over to join her. "I figured you'd want to talk," she said softly.

"And I bet you'd like to reminisce," Jack replied, to which Gzifa laughed again.

"Quite true," she agreed.

So Jack sat down and poured Gzifa a drink. And together, they relived the events of the day, one from the perspective of having just experienced them, and the other having lived almost a century and a half since the events. And Jack found a deep satisfaction in their talk, sharing a secret only one other person in the world would know about...

Key to Everything

My most vivid knowledge of my beginnings are the days where I shared one body with another. But there are memories that precede those times. Faded. Dim. They come to me in small pieces; mere fragments of what I know to be truth.

I came from... somewhere else. That world is gone now; consumed by creatures my new home can hardly comprehend. I died to escape that world, and in doing so I found myself adrift in darkness. I floated onward, a single soul amid millions in a vast emptiness, for time unknown. All was silence and my memories slipped away. Eventually only two things remained certain in that endless night; I knew my name, and I knew my purpose was yet unfulfilled...

I was so very weak when I was at last pulled free of those dark waters. I lingered for a time as nothing more than a quiet voice in my new companion's mind. But I could see through his eyes. Color returned. And I felt the depths of his emotions as he steadily revitalized me.

Even after regaining a body of my own, I found it difficult to separate myself from him. We had become two halves of a whole, sharing everything. Hopes. Fears. Ambitions.

Love...

It was hardest of all to part ways with him, and I vowed to one day return to his side. But the woman we cared for had to go back to her own life, and he could not follow her there. So I went in his stead to keep her safe, until the time came that her own work was complete.

Coming to Vocari was an awakening of sorts for my fractured memories. This land reminded me of home everywhere I looked. And though I had duties to perform in my new life, my original purpose emerged in full-force as well. Those beings that destroyed my first home were still out there, searching for other worlds to devour. And I was the only one left with the power to stop them...

* * *

"No," Redwynd said firmly. "Absolutely not."

It was the reaction I expected from him, even if I had been hopeful for a different answer. We barely knew each other in this age, so it was all right for the Sylvan king to have his misgivings. Add in my close ties to Gzifa, who he seemed to dislike down to his core, and my fate was pretty much sealed.

"I only need a moment to speak with her," I pressed stubbornly.

Redwynd shook his head. "Taur'Arnor is *closed* to the Deep elves. I will not open the borders, even for you."

I sighed. "You know, technically I'm not a Deep elf..."

Redwynd wasn't amused by my playful tone. "No," he agreed. "You aren't even a real *elf* at all. That doesn't exactly help your case." He sat back, watching me from sharp eyes. "My people have been cautious since the Reversal. I'm not about to invite in an outsider, let alone lead one to our most sacred grounds. That would be a betrayal of all the trust they have placed in me for the last twenty years."

I sighed again. "Fine," I conceded. "I'll have to look elsewhere, then..."

As I stood to leave, Redwynd tilted his head to the side. "Why are you seeking an audience with a goddess anyway?"

I offered him a smile. "I might have been willing to tell you if you were willing to grant me time with Aralee. But since you have refused, it's really none of your business."

His brows drew together. "It's my business if whatever you're attempting could affect this world," he argued.

I turned away. "Oh, it will," I assured him. "But not in the way that you think."

Before he could respond, I severed my connection to the room he sat in at the tavern in Leviathan. The image of my body vanished before his eyes, and my consciousness returned to my physical form in Mith'Arnor. I blinked around, taking in the tapestries that lined the walls and the morning sun that trickled in from the balcony.

The bed moved as the figure beside me realized I was once again present. I turned to regard her, getting caught in her icy blue eyes.

"Well?" Gzifa asked softly. "How did it go?"

"As you predicted it would," I told her with a small smile. "I suppose I should just listen when you say something is a lost cause."

She frowned. "Was it because of me?"

I shook my head. "I was polite and stayed out of his thoughts, but I am fairly certain he refused because it was *me* who asked," I said gently. I reached out and stroked her cheek. "Don't trouble yourself over it. There are other options."

Questions burned behind her eyes. I could hear them clearly, though she did not ask them aloud. She longed to know what it was that I was hoping to accomplish. But I did not want to hurt her by explaining it in full.

For my plans to come to fruition, I required someone of great power. Normally, I would not have looked farther than the woman at my side, though Gzifa still buried much of her strength behind a wall of self-doubt. But in this particular matter, Gzifa would be incapable of helping me anyway. So I was forced to look beyond what I knew. And what was left to me *had* to be a goddess...

"With Aralee out of reach, where will you go next?" Gzifa inquired.

"Soliana or Ulara would be my next best bet," I said slowly. "Vivirene is too unpredictable, and I'm not sure that Chloe would even answer my call."

"Soliana hasn't responded to a summons in centuries," she mused. "But Ulara is usually happy to aid those who seek her out."

"Then she is who I will try next," I said firmly. "Do you think you could help me gain an audience? If not with Ulara directly, then with the Maidens?"

Again, her mind flooded with questions. But Gzifa did not voice them. She trusted me to do what I must, and to tell her as much as she needed to know. "I'll do what I can."

I took a breath, leaning forward to press my forehead to hers. "I know it's frustrating to do this without an explanation," I told her. "And I am very grateful for your help. I promise, all will be made clear in time. And I hope you do not resent me for what I am doing."

She chuckled. "How could I ever resent you? You aren't endangering Vocari, are you?"

"No," I said quietly. "In fact, I'm hoping to do the exact opposite..."

She gave me a quick kiss. "Then I doubt you need to worry about upsetting me."

I sighed. That remained to be seen.

* * *

It was my first visit to Ebongate. Any other time, I might have had more interest in exploring the city. But today, I had a job to do, and my mind was on what I would say if I managed to meet with a goddess.

Gzifa led the way to the Temple of Ulara, her steps sure and a smile on her face. It wasn't often that I felt such joy from her, and it made me happy, too. Gzifa's demeanor had changed so much since our arrival in Vocari, and I cherished the little moments where I could catch a glimpse of her as she was in Cadence. When we were all together...

The Temple was exactly as I knew it would be; exactly as Gzifa always pictured it. The sight put me at ease and I eagerly stepped into the cool interior behind my companion. A priestess waited for us just inside. I recognized her as well from Gzifa's memories. Seler'Anoron.

"We've been expecting you," Anoron said pleasantly as Gzifa hurried to embrace her.

"You have?" I asked in surprise. We had not sent word ahead of our arrival.

Anoron gazed at me knowingly. "You are the one known as Dreamwalker, are you not?"

Raising a brow, I nodded and bowed. "You may call me Theofred," I said politely.

She smiled. "Ulara sent a vision to Seler'Elena, telling her you would be coming," she informed me. "The goddess is never mistaken in such matters."

"Where is Seler'Elena?" Gzifa asked.

"She's in her study. Come; I will walk with you."

As we moved through the Temple, Anoron and Gzifa chatted happily. I stayed quiet, looking around with wonder. The place was so very familiar to me, though I had never been there in person before. I knew I could navigate the halls with my eyes closed if I wanted to. Just as I knew when we arrived at the private chambers of the High Priestess in charge of the Temple.

* * *

Encouraged by the very goddess I had come to see, Elena was more than happy to aid me. That evening, Gzifa and the Maidens of Ulara gathered in the heart of the Temple. They formed a circle around me and sang as their High Priestess guided me into the realm of the gods. I gazed at Gzifa one last time before closing my eyes, and when I next opened them the Temple was gone.

I stood on a silver beach beneath an endless starry sky. The moon hung impossibly close overhead, full and magnificent. The ocean roared as the waves stretched out to greet me. And a sense of utter serenity fell over my mind.

"Greetings, Theofred Dreamwalker," said a whispering voice behind me.

I turned to regard the speaker, my breath catching in my throat. Hers was another face I knew from Gzifa's memories. Impossibly tall, gracefully beautiful, with silvery hair and eyes like a midday sky. A smile played at her full lips as she studied me.

"Ulara," I said softly, bowing low before her. "Thank you for deigning to speak with me, Goddess. I am honored."

"How could I refuse?" she asked smoothly. She took a few steps forward and ran a hand under my chin. "You are hardly like the other mortals that seek me out. In fact… you aren't *mortal* at all, are you?"

I swallowed, surprised to feel a shiver run up my spine at her touch. "To be honest, I'm not sure what I am, my Lady," I told her in a hushed tone.

"But you do know what you are here for," Ulara said serenely. "So tell me."

I took a breath. "I wish to extend my experience in this great weave of life," I explained quietly. "Specifically, I want to have children of my own… But, as you can see, I am not a being of flesh and blood. I cannot create new life of myself, and no mortal woman could ever conceive from me."

"And so you request the help of the Divine," Ulara intoned, beginning to circle around me.

I nodded slowly. "I have a plan that would involve the rebirth of past souls into new bodies. I would happily offer of my own power, but I would also require a 'mother' to provide life essence and a physical form for these children to inhabit."

As she came back into view, she smiled. "Why?" she asked. "You do not do this on a whim, or simply to give old spirits a new life. And you certainly don't do it just to pass on your name. There is a deeper reason."

I knew I couldn't hide from her. And unlike with Gzifa, I couldn't just choose to keep my secrets. Not if I hoped to gain her help in the matter. So I told her the truth.

"There is a great threat within the universe. One that endangers *all* worlds. I escaped it once, but my home was lost. There will come a time when that horror comes here, as well. And there is no force on Lapus or among the gods that could stop it…"

"You believe these 'children' of yours could provide a solution?" Ulara inquired.

"I know they could," I told her without hesitation. "I carry the key to our survival within me, but I cannot wield it. That power must be passed on to another. But with my new body, I am incapable of imparting it to anyone without help. Your help, Goddess. In that regard, I've come to make a deal with you."

"Hmm…" Ulara turned away, tilting her face to the sky above. She was silent so long that I was sure she would refuse. But when she spoke again, her words were musing, thoughtful.

"You speak truth, Dreamwalker, and I cannot refute that.

This threat you mention is already known to the gods, and we have long sought a way to counter it. But there are many differing futures that come into play should I choose to work with you. So many possible outcomes... Still, I think I will agree to this deal of yours, so long as you allow me to set some rules of my own."

"Rules?" I asked.

She turned back and nodded. Her eyes were alight with her own ideas and desires, but I could not see into her mind to determine what she was thinking.

"I will grant new life to two souls, which you will retrieve for me. But they will be souls of *my* choosing," she said firmly.

"That is agreeable enough," I told her.

Ulara smiled. "And second; I will only do this if you agree to do something else for me, as well."

"And what would that be, Goddess?" I inquired, suddenly nervous.

She waved a hand. "You require a 'mother' for this to work. I will fill that role for you. But in return, I will also require a mother from you," she said slowly. "*My* mother."

I frowned. "Morwen?"

"Maranwë," she corrected softly. "She remains buried beneath the corruption that has overtaken her. I would have you free her from that darkness, at long last. It will take a great amount of power, and a very delicate touch, but it *can* be done." She smiled again. "I help you. You help me. Is that still agreeable?"

I hesitated, seriously considering it. "Something tells me such an endeavor will take time," I murmured.

"You need not wait for my end of this deal," Ulara remarked. "I will do my part the moment you have the souls in hand. All I need is your word that you will return the favor when the time is right to do so."

"Then it's a deal," I told her with conviction. "Though I am not yet sure how I will manage it, I vow to do my part."

Ulara nodded. "You will not have to do it alone," she assured me. "In fact, it will be best if you seek aid in the matter. But take care not to reveal too much. Morwen will not be easily fooled. She must be made to believe that she is in control, right up to her end. I have already spoken to my father and he has agreed to help, but even he will not be enough."

"I'll need a team then," I said slowly, considering my possibilities. "And they can't all know the plan; at least not right away..." I met her gaze. "I would take your lead on this, Goddess, if you have any ideas."

"I do," Ulara confirmed. Then she opened her mind to me.

Faces flashed by in a blur. Gzifa and Endor. Danica. Loki. Redwynd. Edwood... I could see their power coming together, and an array of artifacts that would be needed. And I could see what needed to be done in order to set them all on the same path. It would not be easy or pleasant, and some of it truly pained me to witness, but Ulara's confidence promised that the choices I made would save far more people than they endangered. And if I played my cards right, no one I loved would die...

"Can you do it?" Ulara asked quietly.

"Yes," I said firmly. "Just show me where to start."

"You will begin by introducing yourself to Morwen," the goddess said shrewdly, "by collecting the first of your two souls."

I opened my mouth to question, but she explained before I could ask.

"You are one of three unique beings within this world, Theofred Dreamwalker. The power you possess does not belong here. It is very rare and incredibly valuable. Once Morwen senses it, she will stop at nothing to have it for herself. *That* will be the catalyst that sets our plans in motion."

She held out her hand. A silver medallion rested in her palm and she offered it to me. I took it in silence, feeling the pulse of her energy within it.

"This charm will protect you from Morwen," she explained. "While you wear it, you will be out of her reach. And I will be able to work through you in the coming hours, without the need for you to return here ahead of schedule."

I pulled the chain over my head and felt the weight of the silver where it settled over my chest. "I suppose that means it's time for me to go?"

She nodded. "I will use the medallion to send you to the souls you need to collect, when you are ready to begin. Call upon me again when you have them, and we will continue our work. Until then, good luck to you."

* * *

Seler'Elena was the only one left in the Temple proper when I returned to my body. I looked around in surprise, the moon had long since passed from the window overhead, and all was silent.

"They have all gone to bed," Elena told me quietly. "Did you find what you were seeking?"

I raised a hand to my chest. The silver medallion was still there, hidden beneath my shirt. "I do believe I did," I said.

Elena smiled. "Good. It isn't often that Ulara takes interest in the affairs of mortals with such vigor. You are only the second to speak with her directly in the last century. Gzifa was, of course, the first."

She stood and beckoned. "A guest chamber has been prepared for you. Gzifa is already there, waiting for your return. I will take you to her."

"No need," I said politely. "I know the way."

Elena seemed surprised, but she did not question me. With a familiar hand-to-heart gesture, she bowed out of the room and left me to find Gzifa on my own. Sure enough, I located the guest rooms with ease, following memories that were not my own. And as I drew closer, Gzifa's sleeping mind became clear to me. She was dreaming of the other who wore my face. That made me smile, and I entered the chamber in silence so as not to wake her.

Being what I was, I did not need to sleep. I still indulged from time to time, but I much preferred to walk through others' dreams. So as I sat down on the edge of the bed, I carefully slipped into Gzifa's thoughts. I would not disturb her dreams, but I wanted to view them alongside her. And as this was our only way of being close to the one we missed most, I would guard the moment carefully and ensure no other dreams interfered.

I sat there for over an hour, watching as she danced with him beneath three moons. I listened to the easy drawl of his words, loving and confident. And I wished that I could take her back to him for real... But Gzifa still had work to do, and she would not leave Vocari until she knew it was done.

As the dream came to an end on its own, I leaned forward and planted a kiss on Gzifa's cheek. She sighed happily in response, but did not stir. Smiling softly, I waited until I was sure she was lost in another dream. Then I reached for the medallion.

"I'm ready, Ulara," I thought quietly. *"Take me to the first soul."*

* * *

I found myself in a dark room of stone. Rare silks lined the walls and a lavish bed sat to one side. Closer to me, a familiar figure stood over a scrying bowl. I stared at her in silence, my mind reeling.

It was Gzifa, but not as I knew her. This Gzifa was younger, with hair that fell to her ankles and a hungry gleam to her eyes. This Gzifa dressed in a fine gown and adorned herself with precious jewels. A whip hung from her gem-studded belt, its three tails ending in snake heads. I recognized her as the Shadow Priestess; Gzifa as she was before she left the service of Morwen. Gzifa as the villain I had only seen once before when we were still in Cadence...

That meant Ulara had transported me through time. I was in the Zhamar compound in Shri'val.

As I watched, images swam in the scrying bowl and Gzifa's face twisted into an angry snarl. She turned toward me, one hand reaching out. For a moment, I was certain she was reaching for me. But she looked right through me as if I weren't there at all. And when I looked over my shoulder, I found a group of Deep elves chained together behind me. Slaves.

Upon Gzifa's command, the first in the line stepped

forward. Then he shrieked and died. His body crumbled to dust, and his life essence flooded into the scrying bowl. The others cowered in fear, whimpering and clutching each other tight. Gzifa paid them no mind, her attention fixed on the events she viewed in the bowl. And after a moment, she spat out a furious curse and did it again. Another slave died.

I studied Gzifa critically. Even with the sacrifices, it was clear the spell she used was wearing on her, I could see the exhausted desperation on her face. But I also knew she would not stop until she had the outcome she desired. It was hard to see her that way. Twisted. Malicious...

Again something happened within the bowl that was not to her liking. This time, when she reached out to the slaves, she did so with a scream. Power surged in the room and the remaining slaves were instantly caught in the spell. I watched in horror as they all died at once to fuel Gzifa's dark magic. And as they dissolved away, I felt their souls leap toward the bowl.

In that same moment, my amulet grew hot against my skin. One of the souls broke free of Gzifa's spell and hurtled back toward me. It slammed into me with enough force to make me stagger, and I felt it latch onto my own spirit. A quiet consciousness joined my own. Female; terrified and confused. I quieted her with a thought, urging her to sleep, and prepared for Ulara to whisk us both away.

Gzifa's spell flashed. She went rigid for a moment over the bowl. Then the bowl went dark and her eyes rolled back. She slumped to the floor, unconscious. Involuntarily, I took a step toward her. But I could not reach her side before a new presence entered the room.

She came without form, flooding the shadows around me. I felt her eyes on me and her power hung heavy in the air.

"What are you?" Morwen hissed menacingly.

I was pulled away before I could offer an answer. Then Ulara's peace surrounded me once more and I was carried on to the second soul I needed to collect.

* * *

Ulara surprised me with her second choice. I found myself in a dirty alley, surrounded on all sides by debris and foul smells. I couldn't be sure what city I was in, but I knew it wasn't a nice place. There was smoke in the air, cloying and rancid. The mud under my boots came from dirty water thrown out the windows of the encroaching buildings. And there was a sense of sorrow and despair that hung on my mind from the surrounding streets.

For a moment, I was alone in the alley. Then the sound of hurried footsteps drew my attention to a nearby cobbled road. There were shouts, and someone wheezing for breath.

A young man came around the corner. He was human, ragged and thin from malnutrition. His clothing hung loose on his bony frame, and his feet were covered by nothing more than tattered strips of cloth. He staggered toward me, not seeing me at all, and his dark eyes were filled with terror. Sweat beaded his brow and slicked his greasy hair. Behind him, three more men came into view.

They were well-dressed and obviously well-off. Their clothes were clean and their boots were freshly polished. They stalked the ragged man through the muck with leering grins and mocking laughter.

"Please!" the poor man cried desperately. "I haven't done anything!"

"Well that's just not true," said the bully at the head of the pack. His friends snickered. "You made eyes at a Lady. That's not allowed, friend."

"I didn't!" the man whimpered. "I was only resting by the fountain... Her Ladyship offered me coin, nothing more."

The poor man reached the end of the alley. A solid wall blocked his escape onto another street. He backed up against it, clutching at the stone. The three young noblemen advanced slowly, like cats cornering an injured bird.

"You spoke to her," one of them accused.

"Only to thank her for her kindness, my Lords! There's no law against that!"

"Buddy, right now *we* are the law," the leader snapped gleefully. "Now, I'm afraid you'll have to pay for attempting to rise above your worthless station. Daring to address a woman of noble birth as an equal..."

"Wh-what? No! I never-!" The ragged man attempted to move around them, making a break for the open alley beyond.

One of the noblemen launched out a foot, tripping the poor man. As he fell, mud and foul water sprayed the area. It splattered across the fine clothes of the bullies and their loud laughter ground to a halt.

"Now look what you've done!" their leader spat furiously.

"I'm sorry," the poor man begged weakly.

"Oh, you will be!" And the three converged on him, their booted feet stomping him into the mud.

It took far too long for the poor man to die. His bones broke under the force of their kicks. His blood swirled in the muddy water. But what finally killed him was one of the men standing on his head, driving his face into the sludge and holding him there until he suffocated. And all the while, the noblemen laughed at his pitiful struggles. When he finally lay still, they walked away without a backward glance, already discussing their evening plans as if they hadn't just murdered someone.

I watched them go in disgust as my medallion flared. The poor man's soul joined the Deep elf girl's within me. I soothed him, lulling him to sleep, to rest, and felt some of his pain fade as he quieted.

Those nobles... They had everything the world could offer. And yet, they felt it necessary to be cruel to one less fortunate. I looked back to the broken body in the mud, silently mourning a life that had meant nothing. And I was glad that I could grant his soul another chance at a life of dignity...

* * *

I was back within Ulara's Moonlight Shores. The goddess stood before me, her smiling countenance peaceful and welcoming. I bowed before her, still solemn after the things I had witnessed.

"Do not worry, Theofred," Ulara said comfortingly. "Your children will be washed clean of their past selves. They will carry no memories of the horrors they endured."

"I thank you for that, Goddess," I murmured. "Neither of them deserved such an existence..." I met her gaze. "What must I do now?"

She stepped up, towering over me, and leaned in close. Her silvery hair fell around me, brushing my cheek, and her hand caressed my chin once more. "Now, you will give those souls over to me, so that I may do my part," she whispered. Then she pressed her lips to mine.

I am not flesh and blood, and yet I shivered at the kiss. I could feel her power washing over me, threatening to drown me in its weight. And I felt my body respond, falling into that energy with every piece of myself. The two extra souls I carried surged up and out of me, pouring into Ulara, and left me feeling empty inside.

"Hmm..." Ulara backed away, watching me with a new look in her eyes. "This is unexpected."

"What is?" I asked.

She shook her head. "This key you speak of carrying. It did not transfer with the souls."

I frowned. "Why not?"

"Because it isn't there to be passed on."

I stared at her, my mind going blank. "Not there?" I repeated. "But where else would it be...?"

The answer was already dawning on me as I asked the question. If the key wasn't within me anymore, then it had already been passed to another. And in that case, only one person could be carrying it. The one whose body I had shared for a time.

"Eglandir," I murmured glumly. "I must have left it with

him when we separated..."

Ulara sighed. "There is nothing I can do about that," she told me. "I'm afraid I cannot give you what you seek, after all."

"No," I said quickly. "You *can*. I came here for my children. I still want them, even if they cannot become what the world needs. I will take them, and I will uphold my end of our deal as promised."

Ulara's smile returned. "You honor me, Theofred Dreamwalker. Very well. I will give your children life without your key. May their company bring you comfort in your long life."

She turned and motioned to the waves crashing on the shore. I followed her gaze, noting with awe the figures that emerged from the water and stepped onto the beach. They were adults, fully formed but new and lacking the scars that come from aging. The first was female, small and dainty. The second was male, tall and strong. They walked side by side, appearing as Deep elves and dressed in violet robes. And as they drew closer, Ulara beckoned them to her side. They moved as she directed, without speaking or blinking. I could see they were nothing more than empty shells.

Ulara laid a hand atop the girl's head first. "She will be named for me. Karliah Nightingale," the goddess said softly. "In time, she will bring new hope to the elven nations in a way that has not been seen in centuries."

As she spoke, the stars overhead shone brighter and a silvery glow fell over Karliah. In an instant, the girl's eyes sparked with life. She took a gasping breath and looked around in wonder. Ulara motioned to her, then ushered her my way, and the girl stepped up to me with a smile.

"Hello, Father," she said in a high, clear voice as she wrapped me in a hug.

I was taken back by the familiarity of her mind as it touched mine. But I embraced her readily enough, returning her smile with one of my own. "Karliah," I whispered into her hair.

Ulara moved on to the male, repeating the process to grant him his soul. "And following tradition, he will be named for you. Theofred Ravenmantle. He is destined to journey far and become a great hero in his own right. He will discover many powers within the world. And he will one day aid his sister in her own ultimate purpose."

Theofred came to life in the same way as Karliah had, taking in his surroundings with wonder. Then his eyes locked on me and he strode over and offered his hand. I clasped it firmly, grinning uncontrollably all the while. Like his sister's, his mind was becoming clear to me. I could sense both of their intellects, and their strengths.

"You are perfect," I told them proudly before looking back to Ulara. "Thank you, Goddess."

She nodded back to me. "Take them and go in peace," she said gently. "You have time before your own work must begin, so enjoy it. I will call you when all is ready to free my mother."

* * *

Back in the guest chamber of the Temple, it was nearing sunrise. Gzifa's mind was awakening, stirring from her sleep. I sat beside her as I had before, and bid my children to wait outside while I spoke to her. I brushed the hair from her face with a gentle touch. She smiled and sighed, slowly opening her eyes to look back at me.

"How did it go with Ulara?" she murmured. "Did you find what you were looking for?"

I smiled back. "Not everything I was looking for," I conceded. "But she did help me."

"Hmm... And are you finally going to tell me what it was you were doing?" she inquired teasingly.

I sighed. At this point, there was no choice but to explain. Still, I hesitated. I didn't want to chase away her happy smile so soon.

"Gzifa...," I said slowly. "If I'm honest, I didn't tell you before because I didn't want to hurt your feelings..."

That got her attention. She stopped mid-stretch to stare at me in surprise. "Oh?"

I took a breath. "I went to Ulara for something *neither* of us could have managed. Myself because I am not mortal. And you... because you made it impossible for yourself..."

Seeing a frown start to form on her face, hearing her thoughts begin to whirl, the words spilled out of me in a rush.

"I needed divine help in order to carry on my legacy."

"Your legacy..." Instantly Gzifa calmed. There was a twinge of pain in her emotions, but it was quickly buried. Understanding bloomed and she sat up to look me in the eye. "You wanted to have children?" she asked without anger.

I nodded. "I didn't want to say anything... I didn't want to upset you."

To my surprise, she let out a laugh. "Oh, Theofred... You don't need to worry about that!" she assured me honestly. "It's a bit of a surprise, sure, but I could never fault you for desiring such a thing, let alone try to stop you from achieving it." She reached out and cupped my face, her touch tender and her mind filled with nothing but love and curiosity. "I am happy so long as you are," she said. "And Ulara granted your wish?"

"Yes," I said, finally daring a smile. "Twice over."

Gzifa shook her head. "Then where are they? I would love to meet them."

On cue, there was a knock at the open doorway. Gzifa looked past me, her eyes going wide. There was shock in her mind at the sight of two adult elves as my children came into view. But that shock only lasted a moment. Then she was climbing out of the bed to greet them. I trailed behind her, clearing my throat.

"Gzifa, let me introduce you to Karliah Nightingale and Theofred Ravenmantle," I said softly.

They nodded to her respectfully as I said their names. Gzifa took each of their hands in turn, marveling at them.

"This is incredible," she said softly. "You are incredible!"

And I knew she meant it. I smiled more widely. It was all right that my initial goal hadn't yet been achieved. There was time still for that. In the meantime, I agreed with Gzifa. These two, my children, were a wondrous gift; well worth the price I still had to pay.

"I don't know the first thing about being a parent," I admitted to the room in general.

Gzifa laughed. "Then it's a good thing you skipped the baby stage," she remarked.

"Even so...," I murmured. "They are very much newborns within this world. I could use the help in learning to be a good father to them, and in teaching them of their new lives. Ulara can hardly be present for this. They are in need of a mother."

"If you'll have us," Karliah told Gzifa softly, and Theofred nodded.

Gzifa froze, staring at them. Tears welled up in her eyes, though I sensed no sorrow in her. There was only joy in her mind. Joy and a deep gratitude.

"I would love nothing more," she whispered. And I felt my heart warm in an instant.

www.ingramcontent.com/pod-product-compliance
Lightning Source LLC
LaVergne TN
LVHW040914150826
845672LV00007B/2043

* 9 7 9 8 3 7 0 4 5 7 9 1 3 *